ATTACK
OF THE
GOBLIN ARMY

Tales of a Terrarian Warrior, Book One

ATTACK
OF THE
GOBLIN ARMY

AN UNOFFICIAL
TERRARIAN WARRIOR
NOVEL

WINTER MORGAN

Sky Pony Press
New York

Sky Pony Press books may be purchased in bulk at special discounts for sales promotion, corporate gifts, fund-raising, or educational purposes. Special editions can also be created to specifications. For details, contact the Special Sales Department, Sky Pony Press, 307 West 36th Street, 11th Floor, New York, NY 10018 or info@skyhorsepublishing.com.

Sky Pony® is a registered trademark of Skyhorse Publishing, Inc.®, a Delaware corporation.

Visit our website at www.skyponypress.com.

10 9 8 7 6 5 4 3 2 1

Library of Congress Cataloging-in-Publication Data is available on file.

Cover design by Brian Peterson
Cover illustration by Amanda Brack

Print ISBN: 978-1-5107-1682-7
Ebook ISBN: 978-1-5107-1684-1

Printed in Canada

TABLE OF CONTENTS

ATTACK
OF THE
GOBLIN ARMY

Chapter 1:
NICE TO MEET YOU

Miles clutched the copper pickaxe and drove it into a grassy patch of land. It was odd to be alone in a new world. He had always dreamt of being an explorer and yearned to see the world, but as he stood by himself staring at a blue sky dotted with puffy white clouds, he longed for a friend.

He paused for a moment, taking in his surroundings. Miles took a deep breath and eyed the landscape. As he stood in silence, he spotted blue waves in the distance and wondered if it was the ocean. There was so much to explore in this new land. He'd be the first to admit that he was conflicted about being alone. He loved the ability to decide whatever he wanted, but he also wanted to talk to someone.

As he walked toward the blue on the horizon, the water came into focus. Miles was excited to see the shoreline. There were so many places Miles wanted to explore, so many items to craft and biomes to enter, but he wasn't sure of the rules. He feared that somehow he'd break a rule and wouldn't even know he had done it. This happened to him in the past, and it was one of the reasons he had to escape to the world of Terraria.

The walk to the ocean was longer than he envisioned, and he lost sight of the water as he trekked down a narrow path dense with trees.

"I must be in the forest," he told himself.

"Excuse me, are you talking to me?" a voice called out.

"Who's there?" Miles asked, but he couldn't see through the leaves. He only heard the voice mumble, and he tried to find who it came from. "Where are you?"

There was no reply.

Miles clung to the pickaxe. He wasn't ready to battle anymore and he knew the copper pickaxe wouldn't do him much good anyway since it wasn't a very useful weapon for battle. He could use his sword, but it was very basic. There were better weapons he needed to make before he could even attempt to ward off an attack. "Where did you go?" Miles questioned. He second-guessed himself and wondered if he imagined the voice he heard.

"I'm over here." The voice was louder and Miles knew he was getting closer.

Miles raced toward the sound of the voice, until he saw a person with sand-colored hair, dressed in a shirt and jeans.

"Hi." The man introduced himself, "I'm Matthew."

"I'm Miles."

"This is your first day in Terraria." Matthew nodded his head as he spoke.

"How do you know?" Miles was shocked, but he was also aware that he must look like a noob.

"I know everything about you. I'm your guide." Matthew smiled.

"My guide?" Miles questioned.

"Yes, I'm here to teach you about the world of Terraria." Matthew walked toward a tree. "I suggest you start chopping down wood for your house."

"But I don't want to chop down wood or build a house—I want to explore this world," Miles protested.

"If you don't build a house for me, I'll have nowhere to live," Matthew informed Miles.

"Why should I build you a house?"

"Because that is what people do for their guides."

Miles shrugged. "I don't need a guide. I'm fine by myself. I'm going explore the world."

"Well, if you think you can survive in Terraria with a copper pickaxe and a sword that isn't very powerful, you are quite mistaken. I can teach you how to craft powerful weapons."

"I'm fine with my weapons," Miles fibbed.

"Do you have any money?" asked Matthew.

Miles searched his inventory. "No. Do I need any?"

"If you want the merchant to come, you should have at least fifty coins," explained Matthew.

"How do I get coins?" asked Miles.

"Why should I answer that question? I thought you didn't need my help." Matthew walked away as he spoke, his voice trailing off in the distance.

Miles chased Matthew down a shady path lined with trees. "I do need your help. How do I get money? I want to meet the merchant. And I wasn't telling the truth, I do need to craft better weapons. There's no way I can explore without them."

"You'll find coins in a chest. I will help you find a chest and craft weapons, but you have to build a house first."

"Building takes up so much time. I want to explore."

Matthew shook his head. "I understand your enthusiasm for wanting to explore the world but if you don't build a home, you will be vulnerable to many creatures of the night."

"I'm not scared of them," Miles replied.

"They will destroy you." As Matthew spoke, Miles shuddered.

He quickly grabbed the pickaxe and chopped trees for wood. He wanted to build the house as fast as possible. Miles gathered the wood and Matthew directed him toward a patch of land, "You'll also need dirt blocks for the walls and the ceiling."

Miles carefully laid each brick. After a wall was complete, he paused. "I like it. It's beginning to look like a real home. I've never had a real home before."

"Really? Why?" Matthew asked.

"I don't want to get into it." Miles finished the walls and worked on a wooden door. When he was done, he put the door on the house. "I'm done."

"In order for this house to be considered a home, you'll need a chair, a table and a light source," the guide informed Miles.

"A light source? Like a lamp?"

"A torch," Matthew explained.

Miles thought about how to craft a torch when a group of green slimes approached them. Matthew advised Miles to keep his distance, saying, "Slimes won't attack during the day unless provoked."

As Miles grabbed wood to craft a torch, he accidently upset the green slimes. They hopped up and down, Matthew warned him they were ready to attack. Miles's heart raced. He only had a useless sword. Before the slimes had a chance to hop onto his body, he struck the slimes with his sword.

"Help!" Miles cried as he plunged his sword into a green slime. "I'm surrounded."

Matthew shot wooden arrows at the green slimy beasts that surrounded the duo.

Despite the sea of wooden arrows Matthew shot, they were outnumbered. Miles realized he wasn't ready for a battle. He cried out for the second time. Matthew stopped shooting his barrage of wooden arrows and grabbed his sword. "And you thought you didn't need a guide?"

Miles replied with a gasp as more slimes appeared. He was paralyzed with fear, and silently worried his first day in the world of Terraria might be his last.

Chapter 2:
THE SEARCH FOR COINS

Even though they seemed to be losing the battle, Matthew was a skilled warrior. Miles mimicked his moves as he attempted to battle the gelatinous green slimes.

"Gotcha!" Miles yelped as he destroyed two more slimes. Despite gaining confidence during this brief battle, he sighed with relief as he watched Matthew obliterate the remaining slimes.

"We make a good team," Matthew remarked.

Miles noticed coins in his inventory. "What's this?"

"When you defeat a hostile mob, like a slime, you get rewarded with coins," explained Matthew. "And you also get gel, so you can craft a torch, which you should do very soon since it's almost nighttime."

"Okay, I'll make that torch. But I thought you said we *find* coins in a chest," Miles said, annoyed.

"There are many ways to do certain things," Matthew smiled.

"I still don't have enough coins to see the merchant and I want more." Miles counted his coins again; he needed a lot more coins to reach fifty.

"I know a great cave where we could search for chests," Matthew said, standing by the house. "But we have to finish the house first."

Miles put the finishing touches on the house and crafted the torch, but he didn't have enough wood to complete the chair. He traveled back to the forest with Matthew to chop wood.

Matthew looked up at the sky. "It's getting dark. We don't have that much time; we must work fast or else we will be attacked by zombies."

Miles raced toward a large tree, slamming his pickaxe into the bark; he wondered if he should have crafted more powerful weapons before they traveled to the forest. The Slime attack was still fresh on Miles's mind and he feared zombies would attack him as evening set in. He panted, "Do I have enough wood?"

"Almost," Matthew remarked.

Miles picked up the pickaxe, slamming it into a large tree, when Matthew informed him that they had enough wood and they must make their way back to the house.

As they walked toward the house, Miles spotted something in the distance.

"What is that?" Matthew questioned.

"That's an entrance to a dungeon. I'll tell you about it later."

"Later?" Miles urged Matthew to tell him about the dungeon. A dungeon was exactly the type of place he hoped to find on his explorations. With Matthew by his side, he was sure that he'd be able to unearth whatever hidden treasure lay in the spooky dungeon.

Night was setting in, and Miles couldn't see very well, but he spotted someone standing in front of the dungeon.

"I see someone by the dungeon. I'm not sure who it is." Miles stopped to get a better look at the person who appeared to be guarding the entrance. The man had a large grey beard.

"That's the old man. Don't bother with him." Matthew reminded Miles, "It's dark. We can go to the dungeon tomorrow."

Miles didn't listen and sprinted toward the dungeon, when the old man called out, "I've been cursed by Skeletron."

Matthew chased after. "Don't bother with this old man. It's a waste of time. Come back to the house and I'll teach you how to craft weapons, and tomorrow I'll help you find coins."

Miles walked up to the old man. "You're cursed? Do you need help?"

"Free me of the curse, and I'll let you enter the dungeon," explained the old man.

"Maybe I'm strong enough to save you. I just battled multiple green slimes," Miles gloated.

"Can you help me? My master can't be summoned until night, though," the old man told them.

Miles looked over at Matthew. "Do you think we can wait? It's almost night."

Matthew didn't look at Miles. Instead he fixated on the dark sky. "No, it's far too dangerous. It's almost the blood moon. That is serious."

"Blood moon?" Miles questioned. Just the words sent shivers down his spine. "But I want to help this old man."

"Please, no," the old man begged. "You'll just get yourself killed."

Matthew grabbed Miles and screamed, "Run!"

A horde of zombies lurked behind some trees. Miles ran as fast as he could toward the house, barely escaping the zombie attack.

"You have to build the chair to make the house complete," Matthew instructed, but Miles was too nervous to construct a chair. His hands fumbled and no matter how hard he tried, he just couldn't finish the chair.

"You're doing a good job," Matthew soothed Miles. "Take a deep breath. It's almost complete."

"Oh no!" Miles gasped, as a zombie kicked the front door from its hinges.

Matthew grabbed his bow and arrow and sprinted toward the door. Miles rushed outside to join his guide in battle. Three zombies lunged toward them, and they faced the undead beasts under a blood-red sky.

Miles plunged his copper sword into a zombie, and while another crept up behind him, he quickly struck it. As he pierced the beast with his sword he spotted a cluster of zombies in the distance.

"The blood moon makes Terraria a very dangerous place," Matthew said as he shot wooden arrows at the zombies that crept toward them.

A bunny hopped past them and Matthew called out to Miles, "Watch out! The blood moon makes bunnies vicious."

The docile bunny quickly turned aggressive and pounced on Miles, as a zombie lunged toward him. He was powerless. One copper sword wasn't enough. Miles jumped back, trying to shake the bunny from his leg, as he struck a zombie. Miles was ready to surrender when a wooden arrow pierced the bunny's side, and it was destroyed. He didn't have time to thank Matthew, because he was too busy trying to survive the zombie attack.

There was only one zombie left, but it seemed incredibly strong. It stared at Miles with vacant eyes. The blood-red moon provided Miles with some light, as he used all of his strength to destroy the zombie.

"You weren't kidding. The blood moon is serious."

"Look, it's the bride and groom!" Matthew called out.

Two zombies outfitted in wedding attire lurked in the shadows.

"Who are they?"

"They only come out in the blood moon," Matthew said as he used arrows to stop the eternally wedded creatures from approaching.

"And they brought guests!" Miles cried as a group of blood zombies approached them.

Miles's energy was low and as he struck the groom, he worried if one of the blood zombies might destroy him.

Chapter 3:
BLOOD MOON

Sweat formed on Miles's brow. He took a deep breath as the gruesome blood zombies picked up speed, advancing toward him. Miles swung his sword at the groom, as he kept a close eye on the fiery red blood zombies.

Matthew's arrows flew through the air as he shot at the bride. The groom stood behind his zombie partner. "When you destroy the groom, don't forget to get the top hat."

Miles chuckled. He found it funny that Matthew was able to simultaneously teach and battle. He also realized that Matthew was truly selfless and focused on advancing Miles's game rather than his own survival. However, Miles couldn't let these thoughts distract him—he had to concentrate on the battle.

Miles ripped through the groom's tuxedo jacket and repeatedly struck the zombie groom. The bride came to her beloved's rescue by attacking Miles.

With one more strike, he knew he'd destroy the groom, but the bride prevented him from hitting him. Miles's energy was dangerously low, he wasn't sure he'd survive the attack from the bride. She was inches from him when another flood of wooden arrows destroyed her and Matthew called out, "Grab the veil!"

Miles slammed his copper sword into the groom, destroying him. He picked up the veil and the top hat, placing them in his inventory. The feeling of elation from achieving these war trophies was short lived, because within seconds, blood zombies surrounded him. As the blood zombies surrounded him, Miles was distracted by the grotesqueness of the undead beasts. He struggled to pierce their red flesh with his sword.

Matthew's arrows flew through the air, and he raced toward Miles's side. "Keep striking them!" he shouted. "You'll be rewarded with copper coins."

Miles *really* wanted to meet the merchant. He knew after this zombie battle, he might have enough coins to purchase all sorts of vital resources from the merchant. He plunged the sword into the belly of a blood zombie and the impact obliterated the beast. It had dropped something, and as Miles leaned over to pick it up, two blood zombies lunged at him. Their mouths gaped open as they clawed at Miles. He was too weak to fight back. He wanted to crawl over to the dropped item and place it in his inventory, but instead he ripped through two hostile blood zombies with his sword, hoping it would destroy them.

Another flood of wooden arrows from Matthew struck the blood zombies, instantly destroying them. Miles crawled on the ground, grabbed what was dropped, quickly placed it in his inventory, and raced back inside the house.

"We need a new door," Matthew informed Miles. "Get some wood from your inventory and make one fast."

"But the zombies can rip it off," Miles reasoned. "Why should we bother?"

"We don't want to make ourselves that vulnerable. We must build it. We can't be lazy," Matthew lectured his pupil.

As Miles crafted the door, he asked, "What did that blood zombie drop? I placed it in my inventory, but I wasn't sure what it was."

"That was a money trough. I'm glad you have it in a safe place," Matthew commended him.

"Thanks," Miles finished the door and placed it in the entrance. "Now we should be safe."

"Yes, we have to wait out the blood moon. It's pretty intense."

Miles blushed as he asked Matthew, "Do you think I'm an okay fighter? I mean, I've always dreamt of being an explorer, but after battling the slimes and the zombies, I wonder if I have the skills to become a warrior."

"Anybody can become a warrior. It just takes practice. Also, you need better weapons. If you'd like, I can teach you how to make wooden armor, a bow, and a sword."

Miles pulled the wood from his inventory. "Yes, please teach me how to make them."

Matthew gave Miles detailed instructions on how to craft the weapons. When they were finished, Miles asked, "Who was the Master that old man was talking about?"

"The old man," Matthew sighed, "he was talking about Skeletron."

"Who's Skeletron?" Miles eyes widened.

A loud thump boomed through the world, and Miles was visibly shaken. Matthew looked over at him, "I'm glad you have your new sword and armor. Carry it with you. We need to inspect the world. There is trouble brewing outside and we must stop it."

Miles was conflicted. He was excited to use his new sword, but he was also exhausted from the last two battles. Matthew opened the wooden door, and Miles followed him out.

"I don't see anything," Matthew said as he walked slowly around the house. "We have to venture further from home."

"Really?" Miles's voice cracked.

"I thought you wanted to become a warrior? If you do, you must be able to battle anything that comes your way, even things you'd never expect."

"Like that?" Miles shrieked.

Two large eyes, which appeared to be plucked from an unknown source, floated through the sky and flew straight at Miles. He sprinted toward the house and hid behind a wall.

"Use your bow," Matthew called out to Miles.

Miles pulled the bow from his inventory and aimed at the flying pair of eyes. He fumbled with the bow and the arrow missed its target.

"Try again," Matthew said. "They're demon eyes. You can destroy them. You have powerful weapons now."

Miles aimed at the eyes that floated toward him—one arrow struck an eye. "Bull's-eye!" Miles called out.

"Don't get too confident. You still have one more eye to destroy," Matthew warned.

Miles focused on the single eye and aimed, "Gotcha!" The eye was destroyed. Miles was confident he could be a strong warrior, he decided, as he walked back to the house with Matthew.

"You did a good job today," Matthew smiled.

"I'm going to be the best warrior in Terraria," Miles gloated.

"You have natural skill, but that attitude will definitely hold you back," Matthew told him.

They closed the door to the house, and once safely inside, Miles overwhelmed Matthew with a slew of questions about Skeletron.

"I'll tell you about Skeletron, but I also want you to know there are many other powerful enemies to battle in this world."

"Which is the most powerful one?" asked Miles.

Matthew paused. "Um. I guess it's the Wall of Flesh. If you don't battle that enemy you can't move onto the next level."

"The next level? I want to be on the next level now. Forget Skeletron, I want to battle the Wall of Flesh tomorrow. I think I'm okay skipping the lesser enemies."

"It doesn't work that way. You have to build your skills. I think if we help you get the right tools, you might be able to battle Skeletron."

"What tools?" Miles questioned impatiently. "Let's craft them now!"

"Well, you can find the lucky horseshoe, which is very helpful, but you must travel to the Floating Island to obtain it."

"The Floating Island? I'm going there tomorrow," Miles announced.

"You have to defeat Skeletron before you can get there."

"I guess tomorrow is going to be a busy day."

"You can only battle Skeletron at night."

Miles said, "And once I do, I'll head straight to the Floating Island."

Matthew didn't tell Miles that getting to the Floating Island wasn't that easy. Instead he informed Miles of all the weapons he might need to become a stronger fighter. "You must acquire a demon bow or demonite," he told Miles.

"How do I get that?"

"You need to build up your skills by exploring this world and the Corruption."

Miles had so many questions. He knew that he had much to learn, but he was confident he'd learn it quickly. Miles felt that with Matthew leading the way, he'd definitely be a legendary warrior.

"I am going to be the best warrior and explorer. You will be so proud to be my guide," Miles exclaimed. "And tomorrow I'm going to destroy Skeletron."

Matthew smiled, but the mood changed when a message appeared. It read: *A horrible presence is watching you.*

Chapter 4:
THE EYE OF CTHULHU

"What does this message mean?" Miles's voice shook.

"I knew this would happen." Matthew paced the length of the small house.

"You knew *what* would happen?" Miles was annoyed. He wanted answers and didn't like it when Matthew was nervous. He could tell the message disturbed Matthew. He was pacing the room and mumbling to himself.

"It's the Eye of Cthulhu," Matthew explained.

"Is it like the demon eyes?" asked Miles.

There was no time to answer his question. "It's here!" Matthew hollered,

A large eye, similar to the demon eyes, but bigger and more bloodied, floated next to Miles. He panicked. "Matthew, how do I destroy this?"

The eye stared at Miles. He didn't wait for Matthew's response; he grabbed his wooden sword and slammed it at the eye. But the eye floated away, and Miles raced toward it, clutching his wooden sword. He swung at the eye again, but missed. The eye flew higher and Miles couldn't reach it. The eye came toward him with great speed, and Miles felt the energy drain from his body as he slowly faded from the world.

"Miles!" Matthew cried, but Miles didn't respond. He was destroyed. A gravestone appeared.

Miles respawned in the house. He looked around for Matthew. Calling out his name, Miles panicked that Matthew was gone. He sprinted out of the house to look for his friend, but he was nowhere in sight.

"Matthew?" Miles hollered through the blood red night.

Silence.

"Matthew, where are you?" he called out.

Miles thought he spotted a zombie in the distance and his heart raced. He grabbed his wooden sword and lunged at the undead beast, but he heard the zombie call out, "Stop!"

It was a familiar voice. It was Matthew. "Miles, did you think I was someone else?" He stared at Miles holding the sword.

"I'm so glad to find you. I thought you were a zombie." He smiled. "Let's go home."

As they walked home, Miles's attention shifted toward his upcoming battle with Skeletron. "After being defeated by the Eye of Cthulhu I want to prepare myself to battle Skeletron. Can we work on that now?"

"You almost have the resources. However, even if you had an inventory full of demonite, you still couldn't craft any weapons to defeat Skeletron."

"Why?" Miles was irritated.

"You need to meet the merchant to purchase an anvil," explained Matthew.

"I want to see the merchant now, I have a lot of coins from all of those battles. How do we it?"

"I'll show you. But I worry that your biggest downfall is that you lack patience. I don't want you to rush anything. It won't get you anywhere. And perhaps," Matthew paused and then spit out, "it might destroy you again."

"Nonsense," Miles retorted. "The next time I have to battle the Eye of Cthulhu, I will have better weapons and I'll be better prepared. I follow the rules, right? I'm just eager to battle. I want to see the world. You can't truly say that's a weakness."

Matthew smiled, "I like the way you think." He explained how Miles could summon the merchant.

However, fate intervened and before Matthew could instruct Miles on summoning a merchant, another message appeared. This message wasn't quite as ominous as the last one. It read: *The merchant wants to move in.*

Miles was excited to get a note from the merchant, but he sighed, "Can he live here, or do I have to build another house?"

Matthew nodded. "Yes, you do."

"But that will take up time and I want to battle Skeletron."

A stream of light peeked through the window. Matthew walked over. "The blood moon is over."

"That's good news," Miles replied as he searched through his inventory. "But the bad news is there's no wood left in my inventory."

Miles and Matthew set out to the forest to gather more wood to craft the house for the merchant. Miles found a section of land filled with large trees.

"This looks like a great place to gather wood," Miles said as he banged his pickaxe into the tall tree. When he finished the homes, he alerted the merchant that his house was ready.

A man with a white beard wearing a cap arrived. "What a lovely job you did with this house. My name is John. I'm your merchant."

Miles didn't even look up, because he was too busy counting his coins in his inventory. "I think I have enough to purchase an anvil and a hammer."

"Okay," John took out the tools, and Miles handed him the coins. "My first sales and I have a new home. Today is going to be a good day."

Miles walked over to Matthew and asked him how he could use the anvil.

"I will teach you how to craft weapons," Matthew said and smiled.

Miles smiled, too. "Thanks."

Matthew looked up at the sky. "Night is approaching. We have to get ready for your battle. Skeletron only spawns at night."

As the sky grew dark, Miles's confidence seemed to vanish. In a matter of minutes, he would face one of his toughest enemies. He didn't want to admit that he was worried and wasn't up to the task.

"Are you ready?" Matthew asked.

Miles nodded.

"Let's go see the Old Man."

Chapter 5
SKELETRON

"I see the old man," Miles said as they approached the dungeon.

"Once you defeat Skeletron, you'll have unlimited access to the dungeon. This is very important because you will be highly rewarded once he's gone."

"What can I find in the dungeon?" Miles asked. He was excited to explore it.

"There are golden chests and a variety of useful mechanisms, and it's there you will find the key to the Floating Island," Matthew explained. "But there are also many traps and you must be very careful when you're in the dungeon."

Miles was so preoccupied with getting into the dungeon and what he'd discover, that he wasn't paying attention to the Old Man, who was slowly transforming into Skeletron in front of his eyes once Miles had uttered the words "curse." An enormous skeleton head floated above him. Its bony hands were separated from the head. They floated next to Miles and slashed at him. Miles jumped back. He swung his sword at one skeleton hand, but it ripped through his own arm, and he started to bleed.

The mammoth skeleton head floated toward Miles and the skeleton hand slashed him again.

"You must destroy the hands," Matthew ordered. "It will make Skeletron extremely vulnerable."

Miles leapt at the hands. But he was destroyed by the head.

Miles respawned in his bed and waited for Matthew.

"I lost," he said, trying to hold back the tears. Being defeated twice was slowly gnawing at his self-confidence.

"There will be other battles," explained Matthew, "and you can try to defeat him again."

"Can I go back and fight him now?" asked Miles.

"No, tomorrow night."

"But I don't want to wait," Miles protested.

"Miles, it wasn't your lack of skills that failed you, but it was your arsenal of weapons. You don't have strong enough weapons. Without powerful weapons, you will never win."

"But you helped me craft the wooden weapons," said Miles.

"Yes, those are good, but we need better weapons. If we go mining, you can mine for gold and make gold weapons and armor," said Matthew.

"Would those weapons help me battle Skeletron or the Eye of Cthulhu?"

"I'm sure once you have the right weapons, you will defeat both of them."

The sun was beginning to come up and Miles wanted to go mining. The duo set out for a cavern. Matthew led Miles into the cavern's entrance and pointed to a spot. "This is a good place to begin mining."

With his pickaxe in his hand, Miles mined for a while. He was beginning to believe there was nothing in the ground until he spotted ore.

"I think I see ore!" Miles cried out.

"That's gold ore," Matthew confirmed as they inspected the ground. The yellow glistened as Miles filled his inventory with the valuable ore.

His inventory was now brimming. Discovering the ore made him feel much better. He was very sad that he lost to both the Eye of Cthulhu and Skeletron, but was glad to unearth treasures. He didn't want to stop.

"You have enough ore," Matthew explained. "Let's go back and craft weapons. It will help you defeat Skeletron. We need to do this before it gets dark."

The two went to the house and Matthew gave Miles detailed instructions on how to craft gold weapons and armor. Miles was proud of his work, but despite holding a new gold sword and outfitted in shiny gold armor, Miles was still nervous when the sun began to set. He was worried about his battle with Skeletron.

"It's time to go," Matthew informed Miles.

Miles left the house as the sun set, and shook as he walked toward the entrance to the dungeon.

"I see the Old Man," Miles's voice cracked.

"You can do it. I believe in you." Matthew smiled.

Miles walked toward the Old Man and took a deep breath as he spoke the word, "Curse."

The Old Man was transformed into Skeletron and Miles remembered Matthew's advice that he should strike the hands to make Skeletron vulnerable. One by one he used his sword to weaken the hands, but they weren't destroyed. He gasped in horror as Skeletron's head began to spin. The bony head spun fast and Miles knew this might be the end. He clutched his gold sword and hit the spinning head, shocked when his sword pierced the hard skull and Skeletron began losing energy. The weakened hands floated toward him and he pounded against them until they were erased from the sky.

Now that the hands were gone, Miles could concentrate on annihilating the large skeleton head that floated in front of him. It began to spin again, and Miles took a deep breath and swung at the head until it was destroyed.

Chapter 6:
IN THE DUNGEON

"You did it!" Matthew cheered. "That is not an easy task. Maybe you will be a noted warrior."

Miles was shaken from the battle and Matthew's kind words hadn't really settled in, as he took another deep breath. He finally let out a large sigh and said, "Thanks. That was tougher than I ever imagined."

Matthew stood by the entrance to the dungeon and peeked in. "You can enter the dungeon."

"Can you come with me?"

"No, I can't. You'll have to go alone," Matthew told him.

"But it's too dangerous to be out here on your own. It's the middle of the night. You can be attacked by zombies." Miles worried Matthew would be hurt.

"I'll head back to the house. You go explore the dungeon. You worked hard for this and you deserve to explore it and reap the rewards."

As Miles entered the dungeon into a landscape of blue brick, he found himself on a path in a vast labyrinth. As he navigated his way through the tricky terrain, he realized how much he missed having Matthew by his side.

Miles's heart started to race as he walked down the labyrinth and couldn't find an exit. He turned left, but it led him to a patterned brick wall. Miles wasn't sure how to get out of this life-sized puzzle, and he continued down another path, but was also met by another brick wall. As he tried various routes through the labyrinth, Miles tripped on a wire, unleashing a sea of poison darts in his direction.

"Watch out!" a voice called out.

Miles ducked and missed the arrows. "Who's there?"

A woman with red hair slowly walked by him. "Move away from there, I was standing there five seconds ago," she ordered him as she looked at the ground.

"Are you looking for something?" asked Miles.

"Yes." She spotted something on the ground and picked it up. "I found them. My glasses. I can't see without them. It's totally annoying."

"Oh," Miles said. "Well, I'm glad you found them."

The woman put her glasses on and looked at Miles. "I'm Shelly. You're . . . ?"

"Miles."

"You beat Skeletron. You must be a skilled fighter."

"I guess so," he said, "but I'm having trouble finding my way out of this labyrinth. Can you help me?"

"I can try, but I don't know if I can help. I do know that I can help you fill up your inventory with many resources. Do you need wires? I mean, everyone needs wires. You can never have too many. I know these sorts of things because I'm a mechanic."

"I might need wires," Miles said as he scanned his inventory for his coins.

"Where do you live? Do you have a house?" asked Shelly.

"Yes. Do you have a house?"

"No, I don't. Would you—"

Miles interrupted her, "You want me to build you a house?"

"How did you know?" she smiled.

"You're not the first person to ask," Miles laughed. "If you help me find my way out of this labyrinth, I will build you a house. You can meet my other friends who live near me."

"Great." Shelly was excited. "I think we should walk this way." She led Miles down a path.

As they walked, Miles told Shelly about Matthew and John. He stopped talking as he marveled at a large chest. Miles rushed over to the ground and opened it. "There's only a key in here." He was disappointed, but then remembered what Matthew said about the key to the Floating Island. "Wait, will this take me to the Floating Island?"

Shelly looked inside. "That's a golden key. I'm sorry, it won't get you to the Floating Island; I hear that's a really fantastic place. But it will help us open a golden chest. And those usually contain valuable treasures."

Miles placed the key in his inventory and walked down the path, and looked for a golden chest.

"I think I see something," Shelly called out, and Miles raced over to a large shiny golden chest. "Open it," she instructed Miles.

Miles opened the chest. "Wow! A potion of swiftness! This will come in handy. I don't have too many potions."

"Watch out!" Shelly cried.

An indigo slime hopped toward them. Miles grabbed his gold sword, swung, but missed the slime.

Shelly threw a wrench at the slime, and also missed. Miles struck at the slimy pest again, destroying it. The slime dropped a golden key. "Wow, I have another key!"

"We need to find more chests," Shelly remarked.

Miles was excited when they turned and were finally out of the confining brick walls of the labyrinth. They found another golden chest, as well as an exit. Miles unlocked the chest. "These are shoe spikes,"

Miles put them on his feet and sprinted back to the labyrinth wall and jumped up on it. He was amazed when his feet stuck to the wall, and he was pinncd there.

"Awesome!" Miles exclaimed. "I have to show these to Matthew, he's going to think they're really cool. And I bet he'll tell me all sorts of amazing things I can do with them."

"I think I see something even cooler."

A key sparkled on the ground. "Is that—?" Miles couldn't believe it.

"Yes," Shelly smiled. "That is a key to the Floating Island."

Miles picked it up and placed it safely in his inventory. "I have to show this to Matthew. He will be so excited to see I found the key to the Floating Island. I want to go there today."

"Don't forget, I want you to build me a house," Shelly reminded Miles.

"Of course," Miles said. He couldn't contain his excitement, and he wanted to sprint back to his house.

Light filtered in through a hole. "It looks like sun came up," Shelly remarked.

"Great!" Miles exclaimed. "Let's get out of here. I want to go to the Floating Island today."

Miles and Shelly made their way to the door. Miles couldn't get out of the dungeon fast enough. He raced back to the houses, calling out, "Matthew, I found the key!"

Chapter 7:
THE GOBLIN INVASION

Miles panted, trying to catch his breath as he approached the homes. John emerged from his house. He had heard Miles screaming. John looked at Shelly.

"Who are you?" asked John.

"This is Shelly. She's a mechanic. I have to build her a house, but I have really big news."

Matthew walked out of the house. "Miles, what's all the excitement?"

Miles quickly introduced Shelly and then spit out the news, "I found the key to the Floating Island."

"That's fantastic!"

"I want to go today," Miles said.

"I do want you to go to the Floating Island, but I had another plan for today. I think you should go to the Corruption. You'll find valuable resources there that will help you on your trip to the Floating Island."

"The Corruption?" Miles asked.

"You don't know about the Corruption?" John was shocked.

Matthew walked over. "I thought I've told you about the Corruption. We should travel there soon. It's dark and dangerous, but it's a valuable place to find resources. You've defeated Skeletron and now I think we can go there."

"I want to go now," Miles announced.

Shelly walked over. "I thought you were going to build me a house."

Matthew looked at Shelly. "Miles, I see you've met the mechanic. You're definitely advancing in the game. If you build her a house, I promise to take you to the Corruption."

Miles and Matthew set off to the woods to gather wood. Miles was standing next to a tree when he almost dropped his axe because he heard another woman's voice.

"Your house is empty," she remarked.

"For now," Miles replied. "We will return there soon."

"Can you build me a house?" the woman asked.

Miles stared at the woman. Her appearance was unusual. She had green hair, which she wore in a ponytail. He didn't respond and walked over to Matthew and whispered, "Do I really have to build a house for this woman? Who is she? What is she?"

"That's a dryad. You'll want to build her a house. She'll be very useful to you in this world," Matthew replied.

"Why? This woman with green hair is useful?" Miles was annoyed.

"Don't ever judge anyone by appearance," Matthew snapped. "Yes, she has many resources she can sell you."

"Like what?"

"Purification powder, a dirt rod, and many other items. And she's quite helpful when battling mobs." Matthew rattled off a long list of other resources the dryad provided.

Miles shrugged. "Okay. I guess I'll build her a house. I have to build one for Shelly, too."

He walked back to the tree. The dryad leaned against the bark. Miles smiled, "I'll build you a house. What can you sell me?"

"Manners!" the dryad called out. "Don't you want to ask me my name first?"

"Yes, I'm sorry. I'm just distracted. I'm supposed to go to the Corruption and I want to get there before dusk. And I also want to go to the Floating Island."

"You certainly have a lot of plans," the dryad said.

"I guess I do. I'm Miles and what's your name?"

"I'm Lila. And I have a lot of resources I can sell you—I hope you have enough coins in your inventory," Lila remarked as she watched Miles chop wood for her new home.

The trio walked back to the houses, and Miles constructed two small homes next to them.

Miles felt like a construction expert. He had built so many homes, he felt as if he was designing a small city. Each house mirrored the next and was on an adjacent plot of land. Miles entered this world alone, but now he had so many neighbors. After he placed the wooden door on Shelly's house, he walked inside and crafted a table, a chair, and a light source. "I'm done," he announced, and Shelly and Lila thanked him and inspected their new homes.

"Good job," Matthew remarked. "Let's go to the Corruption."

Matthew led Miles toward the meteorite crash site. Miles was shocked at the size of the dent."

"The force of landing creates a large impact," Matthew said.

Miles spotted a purple biome. "Is that the Corruption?"

"Yes," Matthew spoke slowly so Miles didn't miss anything, "you must be very careful there. There are many enemies. You can be destroyed by the Eater of Souls, Thorny bushes, and other seriously vile creatures."

The warning didn't scare Miles. He sprinted toward The Corruption and as he entered the biome, he noticed Matthew wasn't joining him. "Can you come with me?"

"I have one vital weakness," he explained. "If I get—" He paused. "Um, it's best if I don't go. I'll wait for you."

Miles sprinted into the creepy purple biome, keeping a close eye for any of the vile mobs that Matthew warned him about. Miles gawked at a purple sphere that floated toward him. Miles wasn't sure if it was getting ready to attack him. He grabbed his hammer and slammed it into the floating being. A musket dropped to the ground, and Miles placed it in his inventory. Another sphere floated toward him. Miles was about to hit it with his hammer, when he heard cries outside in the distance. Miles sprinted out of the Corruption.

Matthew wasn't waiting for him like he had promised, and Miles was worried the cries were coming from his friends. He raced as fast as he could toward the homes. The cries grew louder and Miles knew his friends were in trouble. As he approached the homes, he saw his friends battling goblins.

Hordes of little green goblins in various shades struck his friends. Miles noticed Matthew off to the side, shooting wooden arrows from a distance. He remembered what Matthew said about being weak, and he shielded Matthew from the goblin attack.

Miles rushed into the center of the attack. The goblins were vicious, and Miles slammed his sword into the numerous goblins that crowded the space between their homes.

"Help!" Lila cried as six goblins surrounded her. "I'm too weak to fight them."

Miles was able to defeat the goblins that attacked him and rush to Lila's aid. Matthew shot arrows at the goblins that were destroying Lila. Miles pounded goblin after goblin. But it wasn't easy. Although no new goblins were spawning, there were almost a hundred of them, but they were no match for Miles and his four friends.

Matthew's wooden arrows shot through the air, Miles used his sword, John threw knives, Shelly threw wrenches, and Lila drained the life from the goblins with her leaf barrier. Together, they used all of their skills to conquer the invasion of the destructive goblin army.

There were a dozen goblins left and Miles was losing energy. He needed water or food to replenish his strength, but he didn't have time to eat. Instead he grasped the sword and hit two more goblins. The goblins rushed toward Miles; Shelly flung her wrench at the goblins, and Miles had to duck to avoid getting hit by the wrench.

"All of the goblins are advancing toward me," Miles cried. He wondered if this was their battle strategy. Maybe they would crowd around him, so

Shelly, John, and Matthew couldn't attack them without hurting Miles. He wasn't sure. His only chance for survival was running away from the goblins and hiding behind the house.

As Miles raced from the goblins, Shelly threw wrenches at the goblin beasts. She destroyed two. John's knives hit three goblins. When Miles saw there were only a handful of goblins left, he sprinted out and used his last bit of strength to destroy them with his sword.

The final goblin was destroyed and the goblin army defeated. Miles was rewarded with a goblin punter. "Wow! An achievement."

Miles wasn't one to make speeches, but he thanked the group for his help.

"We should celebrate," suggested Matthew. "You've done so well in this new world."

"And you provided us with shelter," added John.

Miles looked at Matthew. "You never told me about the goblins. How come they just attacked us now?"

"I didn't think we would be attacked. Someone has to break the Shadow Orb for them to spawn," Matthew explained.

"The Shadow Orb? What does it look like?" Miles wondered if the purple sphere that he broke with the hammer might have unleashed this goblin siege.

"I assume when you were in the Corruption you broke the sphere and that's why these creatures spawned." Matthew didn't sound upset when he spoke, which confused Miles.

"You guys must be so mad at me." Miles felt awful for causing the invasion.

Lila smiled, "Now we know we're strong enough to battle an army of goblins and defeat them."

"That does call for a celebration," said John. "Let's have a feast.

The group prepared for a feast, but when Shelly pointed to a strange man bound to a tree, they stopped the celebration and sprinted toward the man.

He cried out weakly, "Free me."

Chapter 8:
A VISIT FROM THE TINKERER

M iles looked at the teal-colored man. "Are you okay? Who did this to you?"

As Miles spoke, the man broke free.

"Thank you," he exclaimed as he walked toward them. The first person he approached was Shelly. "Hi, I'm Isaac. You must be the mechanic."

"You're the Goblin Tinkerer, aren't you?" Shelly asked.

"That's me," he smiled.

"What's a Goblin Tinkerer? The goblins were vicious and they tried to destroy us. We had to battle them."

"Goblins. How many were there?" he asked.

"Almost a hundred," Miles recalled.

"And there are only five of you. I'm not saying you guys aren't the best fighters in Terraria," the tinkerer pointed out, "but I have to tell you, goblins aren't that hard to battle. I mean they aren't rocket scientists. Well, actually some of them are."

Miles said, "It wasn't an easy battle. They out-numbered us. I thought we were going to lose."

"I appreciate your honesty. But you know what I'd really appreciate?" He walked over to Miles.

"Let me guess. You want me to build you a house?" Miles asked.

"Yes," Isaac smiled, "that would be lovely."

"Fortunately, I have the supplies," Miles said, reviewing his inventory, "so I can build it right now."

Isaac stood by Shelly. "Where's your house? I want to be neighbors."

Shelly blushed and led Isaac to her house. "Miles, you can build Isaac's house right here." She pointed to a plot of land next to her home. "I think he'll be a great neighbor."

As Miles crafted the house, he spoke to Isaac, "I think it's rude that you asked me to make you a house and the only person you introduced yourself to was Shelly. It was like John, Lila, Matthew, and I don't even exist."

"I'm sorry you feel that way," Isaac said and asked, "How can I make it up to you?"

"You know, I am wasting my day making this house when I wanted to go the Floating Island. I have the key in my inventory." Miles installed the window as he spoke.

"You're doing a fine job with the house, isn't he, Shelly?"

Shelly nodded, "Great job, Miles."

"And I will repay you." Isaac asked, "Do you have any coins?"

"How are you going to repay me? By taking my money?" Miles was agitated. He gathered the last bit of wood from his inventory and started crafting a table and a chair for the house.

"How do you plan on getting to the Floating Island?" asked Isaac.

Miles paused and looked at Matthew. "I'm not sure. I have to ask Matthew. He's my guide and helps with everything."

"Matthew," Isaac said, "isn't it true that a pair of rocket boots would be very helpful? You can use them to get to the Island."

"I already have a pair of special shoes. Shelly can tell you all about it. I found them when we were in the dungeon."

Shelly added, "They are really cool. Miles can stick to the walls with the shoes."

"Yes, those sound great, but they won't get you to the Floating Island. My rocket boots can get you there." He insisted these boots would change Miles's life and that they were the only way he could make his way to the island.

"Okay," Miles said, "I'll take them." Miles looked through his inventory. "One problem. I don't have enough coins."

Lila looked at Miles. "I can go mining with you. We'll search for coins."

Miles asked Matthew if this was a good idea, and Matthew replied, "Yes, and I will go too. The more coins and resources you have the better off you'll be."

John said, "When you come back, I have a bunch of other items I could sell you, too."

"Great," Miles declared, "you will accompany me on my mining trip."

Matthew, Miles, and Lila set out on a mining expedition, leaving John, Shelly, and Isaac at home.

Matthew led them to a cave in the forest. "This looks like a good cave to find gold."

Lila was the first one to enter the cave and shrieked, "Help!"

Three cave bats flew toward her. Miles lunged at the bats with his gold sword. Matthew shot arrows.

"Use an arrow!" Matthew called out to Miles.

Miles fumbled with his bow, as Matthew destroyed the cave bats with his wooden arrows.

"Thank you," Lila exclaimed.

"Seeing cave bats when you enter a cavern isn't a very good sign," Matthew warned them. "We have to get out of here quickly. Start mining now."

Miles banged his ax against the ground and was relieved when he spotted a chest.

"Open it," Lila instructed.

"Coins," Miles called out, "I found coins!"

"Gather them quickly!" Matthew screamed, "And look out!"

A cluster of bats flew through the musty cavern; the winged beasts flew rapidly at the group. Matthew barely had enough time to shoot his wooden arrows. Lila created a leaf barrier around her, attempting to weaken the bats, but it wasn't working. Miles filled up his inventory as fast as he could and his heart began to race.

"Miles!" Matthew demanded, "Forget about the coins. We're going to be destroyed."

"Okay," Miles said. "One second. I'll help."

"No!" Matthew screamed. "Now!"

Miles didn't understand why Matthew was so upset. If he was destroyed he'd just respawn, and he didn't get the big deal. However, he didn't want to disappoint his friends. He quickly placed the last coin in his inventory and battled the remaining bats.

Instead of commending Miles on defeating the bats, Matthew said, "Next time I ask you to do something, you have to listen."

As the exited the cavern, Miles said, "What's the worst that can happen? If you get destroyed, you'll just respawn."

Lila was perplexed and asked Matthew with a loud whisper, "He doesn't know?"

"Know what?" Miles asked. "I can hear you."

"It's nothing." Matthew was annoyed.

"If it's nothing, you can tell me," demanded Miles.

The fight didn't go on very long. It was interrupted when Lila wailed, "Oh no!"

Miles stopped in his tracks and pointed at a large block in the sky. "What's that?"

Matthew replied, "It's a meteorite."

Lila cried, "And it looks like it's heading in the direction of our homes!"

They sprinted toward the house, trying to outrun the meteorite, but they knew this might be an impossible task.

Chapter 9:
CRASH

The trio rushed back to the homes. "Are you okay?" Lila asked her friends.

John stood by his house. His gaze was still transfixed on the sky, "It just missed us."

"We could have been destroyed," Shelly clung to Isaac. "It was so scary. I've never seen a meteorite before."

"I'm relieved that everyone is safe," Matthew said. "There's one positive from this experience. Now we can mine the meteorite crash site."

"Where do you think it landed?" asked Lila.

John pointed off in the distance. "It went in that direction. I assume we'll find it over there."

"Before we go," Miles walked over to Isaac and pulled coins from his inventory, "can I purchase rocket boots?"

"Yes." Isaac counted the coins. "You have enough."

Miles grabbed the boots from Isaac's hands. "I'm going to use these now!"

"Not now," Matthew said. "We are going to the meteorite crash site first."

Miles looked up at the sky, "But night will be here soon."

"Remember what I said in the cavern?" asked Matthew. "I told you that you have to listen. I'm your guide and I know what's best for you. You have to trust and believe me."

Miles recalled the incident with the bats and he also remembered the conversation between Matthew and Lila. "I won't go to the meteorite site unless you tell me what you're hiding from me. I know you are keeping a big secret."

Matthew sighed, "I didn't want to tell you this, but we're not like you. When we get destroyed, we don't respawn."

"What?" Miles was horrified.

"We get replaced," Lila told him.

"And when you defeat the wall—" Isaac said, but Matthew shot him a dirty look and he stopped talking.

"When I defeat what?" asked Miles.

"No, I was about to tell you something, but I realize I might not have my facts right. But Lila was right. When we get destroyed, you never see us again," said Isaac.

John added, "But we don't get destroyed completely. We actually do respawn, but in another world and working with another person."

"So, you were a merchant for someone else before me?" asked Miles.

"Yes," John sighed. "I've been a merchant for a lot of people."

"Don't you miss them?" Miles questioned, his eyes filled with tears.

"I do," John replied. "But that's the way it's always been for me. However, I try to survive as long as I can in one world. I don't want to start over and have a new person build me a house. And I don't say this to just anyone, but I really like this group of people and I hope we can work together for a very long time."

Miles began to feel protective of the group. He knew it was his job to watch over them and to make sure they didn't get destroyed. "Thankfully, you weren't hit by the meteorite." Miles also understood the reason Matthew wanted him to join them at the meteorite crash site was to protect them.

"Let's go to the site," Matthew said.

The group let out a collective gasp when they spotted the site near their house. Isaac remarked, "I thought it landed further away. But it looks like we just missed it."

Miles didn't waste anytime. He grabbed his wooden pickaxe, but Matthew stopped him. "You need to use a gold pickaxe."

Miles mined the site, remarking, "This crash site is so much bigger than the meteorite."

Matthew explained, "When the meteorite hits, it makes quite an impact and creates a very large dent in the earth."

"Why does it crash?" asked Matthew.

Lila said, "It usually happens after someone breaks the Shadow Orb."

"Oh my!" Miles shrugged. "Like the goblins. It's my fault, again. I feel awful. This crash could have destroyed you all."

Matthew spoke calmly, "Please don't blame yourself for any of this. It's all a part of the world. You had to break that orb. If you do nothing, nothing happens. If you do something, you never know what might happen. If we didn't mine for gold, you'd never be able to mine at this site. Your other pickaxes weren't strong enough and now you have a gold one. You are advancing and this is all normal."

"I guess that makes sense," Miles replied and looked down at the ground. "Should I pick up this brown ore?'

"Yes, that is meteor ore, it's very useful," Matthew explained.

Miles filled his inventory with the ore, and asked, "When can I go to the Floating Island? Do I have enough ore?"

Matthew inspected the crash site. "Just a few more bars of meteor ore and you'll be fine. You'll be happy to have a bunch in your inventory."

As Miles placed the last pieces of meteor ore in his inventory, he looked at the untouched rocket boots. He picked them from his inventory.

"Can I put these on now?" asked Miles.

Matthew nodded.

Miles put one boot on and then the next, and his friends crowded around him.

Lila said, "You have to find that lucky horseshoe."

Shelly said, "Tell us everything you see there and report back every detail."

Isaac said, "Those boots are sure to get you there."

Matthew said, "Don't forget the key. And also be on the lookout for harpies."

"What are those?" Miles asked, but he couldn't hear Matthew's response; the boots had already catapulted him high in the air.

Chapter 10:
THE FLOATING ISLAND

The world looked smaller from high up, and Miles could spot the Floating Island high above the trees in the forest. However, before he could reach the scenic island, his boots lost energy and he started falling toward the ground. Miles thought to grab onto some branches, but instead he landed on the water. He put on flippers and swam back to shore.

Miles wasn't ready to give up. He dried himself off and used his energy to jump toward the Floating Island. He flew through the sky and the Floating Island was mere feet from him, when the boots failed him for a second time. Miles landed in a lake and stared at it from the water. He never thought getting to the Floating Island would be so difficult. As Miles stared at the incredible island, he noticed the sun was setting. He had to get to the island and back before nightfall. He feared leaving his friends alone at night. Now that he knew they were extremely vulnerable and wouldn't respawn, he grew quite anxious about their safety.

"I can do this," Miles said to himself. "I will give myself one more try. If it doesn't work out, I'll just head home."

Although Miles didn't want to go home and tell everyone he failed. He knew his friends would understand, but he'd be very disappointed with himself. Miles wanted to make it to the Floating Island. Miles used the boots again. They shot fire from the bottom as he flew all the way toward the Floating Island. He instantly received a message that he earned an achievement, which he couldn't wait to tell Matthew.

Miles explored the island, but stood frozen in terror when he saw a swarm of man-like birds fly toward him.

"Those must be the Harpies that Matthew told me about!"

Miles grabbed his bow and arrow and aimed at one of these strange birds. He struck one, destroying it. Miles shielded himself behind a tree as he continued to aim at the birds. He missed Matthew instructing him during battle.

As Miles struck another bird, he spotted a chest. It looked like the sort of chest that might house the lucky horseshoe, but he couldn't inspect the chest until he obliterated these half-human birds. Miles shot more arrows. He couldn't think of any other strategy, and he was annoyed at himself. He didn't deserve to be a noted warrior when he could barely destroy a flock of birds.

More arrows flew through the sky. Miles marveled when he destroyed the final bird. He quickly raced toward the chest. He opened it and found the lucky horseshoe. He cried for joy, but he was so distracted by the find that he didn't notice another cluster of birds fly in his direction. Before Miles could fight back, he was destroyed. There was no one there to see his gravestone. He just faded back to his friends.

Miles respawned in his bed. He was still wearing his rocket boots. Matthew stood above him.

"I see you met the Harpies."

"Are they birds with human heads?" Miles asked, still weak from the defeat.

"Yes," Matthew said. "I tried to warn you about them."

"Even if I heard you, there wasn't much I could do to avoid them. But I do have some good news." He pulled out the lucky horseshoe, "I found the lucky horseshoe. I did want to explore the island a bit more, but I was destroyed."

"You can go back. Now that you know the way," Matthew smiled.

Miles sat up when he heard a loud cry. "What is that? It sounds like someone is in trouble!"

Matthew sprinted to the door, and as he opened it, he cried, "Goblins!"

Chapter 11:
REALITY BITES

Miles raced from his house, running past spiky balls Isaac threw at the goblins. The balls hit the goblins, weakening them, and then the balls would vanish. Miles grabbed his gold sword, slaying as many goblins as he could. This goblin siege was larger than the last and now that he knew his friends wouldn't respawn, he knew he had to defeat these green enemies.

Lila protected herself with the leaf barrier and drained energy from the goblins, but it wasn't powerful enough. Miles ran to her side to help her. Hitting any goblin that stood in his path, Miles was quickly diminishing the goblin army.

Matthew stood by his home, shielding himself and shooting wooden arrows at the goblins. Shelly threw as many wrenches as she could at the goblins. Miles was exhausted, but he couldn't give up.

There were signs that the goblin army was weakening, and it wasn't long before they destroyed them. He struck three more goblins, ripping into their green flesh and annihilating them.

"We can do it," Matthew called out weakly.

Miles worried about Matthew and sprinted toward him as John called out, "Help!"

John was throwing knives at the goblins, yet his weapons weren't as powerful as the goblin army. They were inching toward John in great numbers and were intent on destroying him. Miles was torn. He wanted to help all of his friends, but he knew that was impossible.

Shelly threw wrenches at the group of goblins that charged at John, obliterating half of the troops that headed toward him. John unleashed a sea of knives as they pierced through the goblin's bodies, destroying them; Miles defeated every goblin that made its way toward Matthew.

"They're gone!" Isaac exclaimed. "I told you they were easy to defeat."

"Easy?" Miles questioned. "I hope you're joking."

"Ah, come on. You can't say they were that hard to get rid of. I mean there must have been over a hundred of them and there are only six of us, right?"

"I thought that battle was tough," Lila said.

"You're a very skilled fighter," John looked at Miles.

Matthew said, "Miles wants to be the most skilled warrior in the world."

Miles blushed. "Guys, I do want to become a better fighter, but I see it's not as easy as one would think."

"Who would think it's easy? That's crazy," remarked Shelly. "Our enemies are crafty and wise, they aren't easy to defeat."

"Except for the goblins," added Isaac.

"Well, I disagree. I think the goblins were hard to destroy," said Lila.

Miles said, "Not to change the subject. And I don't want to gloat, but I did get to the Floating Island."

"I knew those rocket boots would get you there. I sell good products," said Isaac.

"Yes, they did the trick," said Miles. "And when I was there I found the lucky horseshoe." Miles took it out of his inventory and showed the group.

"Wow!" Shelly exclaimed. "What a fantastic find!"

Miles looked at Matthew. "I do want to defeat the Eye of Cthulhu, but what should be my next challenge? I want to advance."

"If you really want to advance," said Isaac, "you have to destroy the Wall of Flesh. However, you know that once you do your friend here is—"

"Stop!" Matthew demanded as he interrupted Isaac.

"What? Don't stop, Isaac," protested Miles. "What are you talking about? What friend?"

Lila looked at Matthew. "You keep important information from Miles. I know you're his guide, but if you really want to be a good teacher, you have to tell him everything. It's not going to do you any good keeping major secrets from him."

Miles was annoyed. "Seriously? Again? Matthew, I want to know everything."

"If you want to know the truth," Matthew took a deep breath, "once you summon the Wall of Flesh, I'm destroyed."

"And a new guide spawns?" asked Miles.

"No," Matthew replied. "Nobody else spawns. I don't get replaced. You will be strong enough that you won't need a guide anymore."

Miles was just processing the idea that once one of his friends were destroyed, they'd go into another world, and he'd meet a new mechanic, tinkerer, etc., but this news about Matthew gone to him forever was entirely different and earth shattering.

"This can't be true." Miles's eyes swelled with tears. "What will happen to you? I need you."

"Like the others, I will go into another world and will be the guide for a new person, but you will be on your own. You will have enough knowledge to make it through the world without me."

"I don't agree. I will never defeat the Wall of Flesh. I will live with you guys forever."

"But then you'll never get to hardmode," Shelly explained, "Everything's harder there, but there are a lot of great challenges, too."

"That is meaningless to me," remarked Miles. "Without you, nothing matters. It just won't be the same."

Matthew said, "The same? You're speaking nonsense. You told me with great confidence that you want to be one of the most famed warriors in this world, and I believe you can achieve it. If I'm the one holding you back, then I failed as a guide."

"But I'll miss you," Miles sniffled.

"I'll miss you too, but that's a part of my job. I teach people how to survive and when they prove they're strong enough, I help another person."

"I don't want you to do a bad job, but—" Miles wept.

"It's normal to feel this way," Shelly comforted him.

"Yes, I know I'll miss Shelly when she's gone," added Isaac.

"Hey, you won't miss anybody else?" John called out to Isaac.

Even Miles chucked, but there was no time to think. Lila accidently incited a group of slimes and they were under attack.

Miles brushed the tears from his eyes and sprinted toward the slimes with his gold sword, striking the gelatinous beasts, and grabbing gel as each one was struck with a fatal blow.

As he slayed the final slime, he didn't have that sense of pride that he usually felt from battle. He felt empty. Miles was walking back to the house, when Matthew hollered, "Look behind you!"

Chapter 12
ZOMBIE ATTACK

Miles was so distracted by the slime invasion, he hadn't noticed the sun had set and zombies were spawning. With Matthew's warning, he turned around and spotted six zombies inches from him. Fresh from his victory with the gelatinous wormy slimes, Miles pierced two zombies with his gold sword, as his friends battled by his side.

The gold sword ripped through two more zombies, and with one final strike, he destroyed the last remaining zombie. The gang sprinted back toward their homes.

Matthew closed the door. "We have to keep a close eye on the door. There might be more zombies tonight."

Miles nodded. "I'll watch out."

Matthew commended Miles on his swift zombie battle. "Not many people could stop a zombie invasion as skillfully and quickly as you did. Miles, you have a true skill in battle and you can't pass it up. I must prepare you to battle the Wall of Flesh."

"But once I summon the Wall of Flesh, I'll never see you again." Uttering those words left Miles feeling heartbroken.

Matthew explained, "Every good teacher wants to see their students succeed."

"Do you think I have what it takes to defeat the Wall of Flesh?"

"Yes, but not yet. There are still many other skills you need to perfect and weapons to craft."

"I know I've said this before, but I'm really going to miss you," Miles looked at Matthew, his eyes once again filled with tears.

"I'll miss you too, but I'll be happy knowing what you are accomplishing in the world. I know you're going to do something great."

Miles's heart swelled with pride. He never imagined he'd do something great, and Matthew truly believed in him. Miles decided he'd try to learn everything he could to prepare for his battle with the Wall of Flesh and his subsequent new life on hardmode.

"I think we should go back to The Corruption," suggested Matthew. "You need to acquire demonite."

"Why?"

"You have to craft a demon bow."

Miles asked, "Is there any other way to get demonite?"

"Yes, from the Eye of Cthulhu. If you destroy it, you will get demonite," explained Matthew.

Miles recalled the failed battle with the Eye of Cthulhu; he was nervous for a second one. Although he had perfected his fighting skills, he was still nervous about battling these insidious floating eyes.

Matthew shrieked as a zombie tore their door from its hinges. Cries were heard outside the house.

"It sounds like Lila is in trouble," Miles said as he banged into the zombie who stood in their entranceway, instantly destroying the beast.

Matthew shot arrows at the zombies clustering around their house, as Miles sprinted toward Lila.

"Help!" Lila cried as six zombies surrounded her.

John threw knives at the zombies that attacked Lila, but he only struck one of the undead beasts. Miles leapt at the zombies, repeatedly striking them with great force, and annihilating them one by one.

"Oh no!" Isaac yelled. "There are more zombies!"

An army of zombies marched in their direction. Miles sprinted toward the army of zombies, lunging at them, but there were too many zombies, and his friends' weapons were weak in battle, and Miles slowly faded away.

"Miles!" Matthew cried, as Miles's tombstone appeared.

"We'll have to battle these on our own," Shelly hollered and unleashed a flood of wrenches at the zombies.

Isaac threw spiky balls and, using all of their collective powers, the gang attempted to stop this zombie army from destroying their newly crafted, small, peaceful town.

Miles respawned in his bed, jumping up as he heard his friends cry for help. As he raced from the bed, an ominous message appeared: *An evil presence is watching you.*

He knew this was a message from the Eye of Cthulhu, but he had to help his friends. They couldn't survive the zombie attack. Miles sprinted toward them, striking every zombie he could before the evil eye spawned.

"Miles!" Matthew hollered. "It's here!"

Miles gasped as two large eyes floated toward him. The pair of eyes stared at him, as he took a deep breath and jumped toward the eyes with his gold sword. He tried to block out the sounds of his friends' cries, but it was nearly impossible. At any moment one his friends could be destroyed and ready to respawn in another world, but he couldn't help them.

The eyes floated toward Miles, ramming into him. His health decreased. Miles struck one eye with the sword, but it made no impact. He leapt at the other eye, slamming his sword against the gruesome eye, which looked as if it had just been ripped from someone's head. Miles wasn't weakening the eyes and was worried.

"Miles," John called out as he shot knives at the zombies. "Use the shuriken I sold you."

The day before Miles had made a large purchase from John. The merchant convinced Miles that he needed all sorts of unusual weapons. Miles thought the shuriken would be a useless purchase, but he was wrong. As he grabbed the star-like weapon and flung it at the eye, he marveled as it considerably weakened the bloodied eye. Miles leapt at the eyes with his gold sword, pounding into them until they were destroyed.

He was rewarded with an Eye of You Achievement, but this wasn't a celebratory event; his friends were slowly losing the battle with the zombies, and he had to race toward them.

"Grab the demonite!" Matthew shouted at Miles. "The Eye of Cthulhu dropped it on the ground."

Miles picked up the demonite drop and returned to the zombie invasion. Confident from his victory with the tricky and powerful Eye of Cthulhu, Miles slayed the zombies until his friends were safe from the creatures of the night.

Everyone thanked Miles for his help. Matthew said, "It's been a long and awful night. Although you battled well and received an achievement."

"And saved us," added Lila.

"It's time to get some sleep. In the morning, we'll travel to the Corruption."

Chapter 13
EATER OF SOULS

"Do we have to travel to the Corruption? After defeating the Eye of Cthulhu, didn't I get enough demonite to craft a demon bow?" Miles questioned.

Matthew replied, "You might, but we should still travel to the Corruption. I don't want you to be afraid of that biome."

Miles couldn't sleep, he was nervous about the trip to the Corruption. The last time he traveled there, he broke the Shadow Orb, which unleashed goblin invasions and launched a large meteorite, one that narrowly missed crashing on their homes. He wasn't sure what he'd do on the next trip. If he asked Matthew about the Corruption, he'd probably just say something vague, telling him that this was all a part of learning and growing, and he had to face challenges or he'd accomplish nothing. The sun shined through their small window, and Miles felt a lump in his throat and a pit in his stomach; he wasn't ready to travel to the Corruption, but he had no choice. Matthew stood above him. "Ready to go?"

Miles nodded. He wore his gold armor and trailed behind Matthew as they walked past the large meteorite crash site and to the purple Corruption.

"Are you sure we have to travel to the Corruption today? I don't feel like I'm ready." Miles made one final plea to cancel their trip.

"Yes," Matthew replied. "There is nothing to worry about. You've done such a great job battling the zombies and the Eye of Cthulhu, this will seem easy in comparison."

Miles didn't agree. He wished there was some sort of distraction to stop them from traveling to this creepy dangerous biome. As they approached the entrance to the Corruption, his wish was granted when a voice called out, "Hi, looks like you're in need of a cure."

"A cure?" Miles stopped to stare at a man with a red beard, wearing a yellow helmet, and carrying all of his belongings in a bag tied to a stick. "Who are you?"

"I'm Jack," he smiled proudly. "I have dynamite. It's my own recipe for whatever might bother you. It can cure anything."

Miles didn't know what to make of this funny little man. He eyed him and looked over at Matthew. "What should I do?"

"Introduce yourself," Matthew ordered. "This is a demolitionist. He's a very useful person to know in this world. Demolitionists have all types of explosives, which are potent weapons when battling hostile enemies."

"Will they help me battle the Wall of Flesh?" asked Miles.

"Dynamite and grenades will help you battle anyone. I've got something for everyone. What do you need?"

Miles paused. "Um, I don't know."

"Okay, here's a better question. How much do you got?" Jack perused his inventory, organizing items by price.

Miles stared at Matthew. Matthew said, "I'm Matthew and this is Miles. Miles needs grenades."

Jack pulled a bunch of grenades from his inventory. "Here you go. Good choice, they're da bomb."

Miles handed him some coins and said, "Thank you." He placed the grenades in his inventory.

"You know how you can really thank me?" Jack asked with a sly smile.

"I think I have an idea," Miles chuckled. "Do you want me to build you a house?"

"Wow, how did you know?" Jack exclaimed. "Yes, that was exactly what I wanted. I think we're about to start a great friendship."

"I will build you a house, but we're on our way to the Corruption, and I wanted to travel there before night. Would you like to come with us?" questioned Miles.

"The Corruption isn't my favorite place, but I'll go for you," Jack replied, and the trio entered the dangerous and deadly purple biome.

Matthew pointed to the ground. "I see a piece of demonite ore off in the distance. You are very lucky. Most people don't find it that quickly. You must use your gold pickaxe to mine for it. It's much too dangerous for us to stay here."

"But I can't do it alone," Miles pleaded.

"Yes, you can. Go to the demonite ore," Matthew said and he left the Corruption.

Miles was alone. He raced to the brick of demonite and banged his pickaxe against the ground, breaking the block of demonite ore from the ground and placing it in his inventory. He had unearthed the bar when a swarm of flying beasts with tentacles surrounded him. Miles quickly lost his health. He didn't have time to trade his pickaxe for his sword, and within seconds Miles's energy depleted. The swarm of flying bug-like creatures destroyed Miles. Again, there was nobody there to see the tombstone, and when he respawned in his bed; Matthew wasn't even at the home.

"Matthew!" he called out, but there was no reply.

As Miles left the house, Lila noticed him. "Aren't you supposed to be in the Corruption? Are you okay? What happened?"

"I was destroyed by a swarm of flying bugs with crazy tentacles that shook really fast. I had no time to fight back."

A familiar voice called out, "That was the Eater of Souls."

Miles smiled. It was Matthew. "What's that?"

"It's a very hard enemy to battle. But don't worry, they only live in the Corruption."

Jack stood behind Matthew and asked, "Since you're done with your trip to the Corruption, can you build me a house?"

The others emerged from their homes, while Miles used his remaining resources to construct a house for Jack.

Matthew stood by Miles. "Did you have enough time to mine for the demonite ore?"

"Yes," Miles proudly displayed his demonite ore.

Matthew inspected the ore. "You still need a little more."

"But I don't want to go back to the Corruption," Miles cried. "I was destroyed within seconds by the Eater of Souls."

Matthew understood Miles's apprehensions, but explained, "You only need a little more demonite."

Miles was finishing crafting a table when Shelly screamed, "Goblins!"

Chapter 14:
THE THIRD BATTLE

This goblin invasion was the worst of the three.

"Oh no!" Matthew screamed as they descended upon the group. "There have to be at least one hundred and fifty goblins."

The green beasts leapt at his friends. Isaac threw a spiky ball at them, striking two goblins. "I told you they were easy targets," Isaac joked, as he threw another spiky ball.

Miles grabbed a grenade and flung it toward the goblins. The loud explosion frightened his friends and destroyed a multitude of goblins.

"Am I right? These are da bomb!" Jack smiled while he also launched grenades.

Lila protected herself with a leaf barrier. Isaac remarked, "Man, why purify the world and use nature when you can just blow it up?"

"I'm all natural," Lila retorted as her leaf barrier weakened a gang of goblins approaching her.

Powerful explosions rocked the town as a flood of knives, wrenches, and wooden arrows shot through the sky. The goblins forces were quickly diminishing. Miles leapt at three goblins with his gold sword, but he was quickly outnumbered. The goblins zapped his energy and he respawned in his bed. Miles was shocked by the eerie silence and worried his friends were destroyed. He sprinted out of the house.

"We were worried about you," Lila said.

"Where are the goblins?" asked Miles.

"We destroyed them," replied Matthew.

Miles was happy his friends destroyed the goblins, but he also felt useless. He wondered how his friends, who were much weaker than him, survived and defeated the goblins, while he was destroyed.

"I am beginning to question if I am truly a skilled warrior," Miles announced to his friends.

"Losing is normal and you can't win every battle." Matthew comforted him.

"But I feel like I've lost every battle. Today I lost a battle with both the Eater of Souls and with the goblins."

Isaac joked, "And we all know the goblins aren't too smart."

"Isaac!" Shelly reprimanded. "That's not nice at all."

"I was only joking."

"Still, can't you see Miles is very upset?" Shelly was irritated with Isaac's behavior.

"Miles," Lila, said standing beside him. "I have an idea. I think you should go back and defeat the Eater of Souls."

"No way!" Miles reasoned, "If I couldn't destroy the goblins, how can I defeat the Eater of Souls? I barely survived the last attack."

Shelly smiled, "Miles, when we met, you were very brave. I want to see the old Miles. The one that was too confident."

Lila added, "I really believe you learn a lot by going back to old battles."

"Really?" questioned Miles.

"Yes, when you repeat something, it helps you prepare for the next challenge. I think once you defeat The Eater of Souls, you will be better prepared to battle the Wall of Flesh," Lila reasoned.

Matthew pointed out, "You have a lot more resources now. I'll help you craft the demon bow."

The sun was setting and Miles knew they were right. He must travel to the Corruption the following morning. It was the only way to prepare for his battle against The Wall of Flesh. He must defeat the Eater of Souls.

Chapter 15:
REPEAT

The Corruption was lined with purple grass and trees. Miles's heart beat rapidly as he clutched his gold sword. He didn't want to miss another stealth attack from the Eater of Souls. He traveled deep into the creepy biome and shrieked when he looked back and didn't see where the Corruption started. He felt trapped in the hostile biome. In the distance, Miles eyed a block of demonite ore and sprinted over to mine. He walked passed a chasm, but didn't dare enter the bowels of the Corruption. He was still a novice, and knew a trip down a chasm wouldn't benefit him until he was on hardmode. However, every time he thought about being on hardmode, he remembered about losing Matthew.

Miles banged his gold pickaxe into the ground, and leaned over to pull out the block of demonite ore, when he spotted a swarm flying toward him.

"The Eater of Souls!" he cried out and quickly switched his pickaxe for a sword and swung it at the creatures.

Miles struck two of the flying beasts, but many remained. They rammed into him, weakening him, but he wouldn't let them destroy him. Miles leapt at a cluster and slammed his sword as their bodies floated past him. The Eater of Souls surrounded him and he was ready to give up, when he remembered the enchanted boomerang he crafted with Matthew. He recalled Matthew telling him to use it when he met the Eater of Souls. Miles grabbed the boomerang and flung it at the Eater of Souls that circled him. He instantly obliterated three flying terrors, and when it returned he swung the boomerang for a second time, annihilating the remaining ones.

Miles raced out of the Corruption to tell Miles the good news, but as he approached the familiar landscape of his town, he heard chilling cries.

"My friends!" Miles shrieked as he sprinted as fast as he could back to the homes.

Miles gasped as he watched the largest army of goblins he'd ever seen overrun their small town. There were countless green goblins attacking the gang and they were running out of energy. The knives, wrenches, spiky balls, grenades, wooden arrows, and leaf barrier were no match for this large goblin army.

"Help!" Lila called out.

"UGH!" Matthew screamed as four goblin surrounded him.

"Oh no!" Isaac hollered when five goblins raced in his direction.

Miles didn't know where to go and who to help first. He attempted to strategize, but there wasn't time. A half dozen goblins sprinted to his side, as he detonated a grenade.

Kaboom!

"Help!" Lila called again, and Miles ran toward her, but was stopped by a crop of goblins. He was out of grenades and used his sword to pound against the goblins

Matthew called out weakly, "Use your spear!"

Miles fumbled with the sword as he grabbed the spear and struck the goblins that cornered him. He looked over at Lila, who was struggling to drain the goblin's energy with her leaf barrier. The barrier was far too weak for battling the multitude of goblins that crowded around her.

"Help!" Lila cried out again.

Miles sprinted to Lila, he banged his spear into the pack of goblins that huddled around the dryad. But it was too late.

"Lila!" Miles let out an agonizing cry.

"It's okay," Matthew called to him. "You can't stop fighting."

"But Lila," Miles wailed. "She's been destroyed!"

"And so will the others if you don't battle the goblins," Matthew said as he shot wooden arrows at the goblin soldiers.

Miles was infuriated with the goblins and used his anger to crush any goblin that walked within an inch of him. He used his spear and his sword to destroy the cutthroat army. Along with his friends, Miles finished the battle. A message was sent announcing the Goblin invasion was over.

Matthew congratulated Miles, "You did it. You stopped the invasion."

However, Miles didn't feel like a hero. "I failed you all," he addressed the group. "I couldn't save Lila."

"That's not your fault," Matthew explained. "The goblin attack was intense."

"He's right," Isaac remarked. "I know I joke that the goblins are dimwits, but they aren't and that attack was lethal. I barely survived and I was armed with spiky balls. Lila was vulnerable."

Nobody could say anything to make Miles feel any better. He was distraught over losing Lila.

Shelly called out, "There's someone in Lila's house!"

Matthew said, "That must be the new dryad. Let's go meet her."

Miles was opposed to meeting the new dryad. "Not me. I'm staying here. I don't want to meet her."

"I know this is tough. But I don't want you to feel guilty about Lila. There was nothing you could do to help her. Remember, you stopped the attack. This is the way our world works, and the more time you spend here, the more things like this will occur," Matthew explained.

"But it just doesn't seem fair," Miles sniffled. "Lila was so nice and helpful."

"I'm certain the new dryad will be the same, but we have to meet her first. It's not her fault she's the one who replaced Lila. I bet she was destroyed in another battle and just landed here, the way Lila will appear in someone else's world," Matthew spoke, but Miles wasn't feeling better. No matter how reasonable Matthew's logic was, he still felt a dent in his heart.

Miles's friends crowded around Lila's house waiting for the new dryad, and Matthew smiled when he saw Miles walk toward them.

Chapter 16:
NEW FRIEND

The new dryad walked out of her house, greeted by all of her new friends. Miles stood off to the side, watching her chat with the others. The dryad stared at Miles, calling out to him, "Hi." She smiled, "Don't you want to join us?"

Miles was embarrassed. He didn't want to appear as if he didn't care about the new dryad, but he was still trying to adjust to how things operated in this new world. "Yes," Miles replied and joined them.

"I'm Isabella," the dryad said.

"I'm Miles."

"I like this house. You did a fine job building it." She paused. "I'm sorry about your friend. I'm sure she was useful to you. I hope I'm also useful."

"I don't miss her because she was useful. I miss her because she was my friend."

"Yes, I know," Isabella said. "But a dryad's most important job is to be useful. I want to provide you with purification powder and all of the tools you need to survive in this world."

"I understand," Miles nodded.

Isabella scanned the group. "Miles, it looks like you've met a lot of useful people. I think it's probably time you move on to hardmode."

Miles looked over at Matthew. "Now? Really? Is she right? Am I ready?"

"Yes," Matthew replied. "You are ready. It's time to summon the Wall of Flesh."

"But you're wrong. I'm not ready. I want to stay here."

"Miles, life is about meeting new people and different experiences. And this isn't all your decision. I'm also ready to leave. Once I teach you how to summon the Wall of Flesh, there is nothing left for me to teach. My job is done. I want to move on to a place where I'm needed."

"But won't you miss me?"

"Of course. We will both miss each other a lot, but we have very different paths. You will become a noted warrior and I will aid another person on their path. I feel rewarded and grateful that I could help you."

Miles understood. He asked, "How do I summon the Wall of Flesh?"

"Good," Matthew smiled. "That's a tough question to ask, but it's also the right question. You've made me very proud." Matthew explained that

Miles had to travel to the Underworld and defeat a Voodoo Demon.

Miles's eyes widened. "The Underworld? The Voodoo Demon?"

"Yes, I know you're strong enough to defeat the Voodoo Demon. And once you do, you must grab the Guide Voodoo Doll."

"What?" Miles head was spinning.

"That doll is vital in summoning the Wall of Flesh."

Miles asked, "Will you be there with me? To give me advice?"

"No," Matthew explained, "my last job is teaching you have to navigate the Underworld, but I can't go there with you. This is something you will do alone. Once you defeat the Wall of Flesh, you'll be on hardmode, and your life will become a lot more challenging and a lot more interesting. I know you'll love it."

Miles didn't focus on losing Matthew. Instead he concentrated on making Matthew proud. He knew he couldn't go into the Underworld without a detailed plan, and Matthew was the perfect person to help him.

"Tell me everything I need to know," Miles said confidently.

Chapter 17:
THE UNDERWORLD

Goodbyes are always tough. But they're a lot harder when you're saying good-bye to your first friend, your mentor, and your teacher. Matthew was all of those things to Miles, and while he tried to hold back the tears, he couldn't.

"I hate long goodbyes," Matthew said, "Just go to the Underworld. You're prepared."

After a week of intense training and crafting weapons, Miles was ready to enter the Underworld deep beneath the surface. He had a list of all his potential enemies and pitfalls. He knew once he got there, he couldn't be distracted. He had to find a Voodoo Demon and start the process of summoning the Wall of Flesh.

Miles's friends crowded around them as they said their goodbyes, and Miles addressed the group. "I will see you guys on hardmode. And I promise to protect you from any hostile enemy we might encounter in this new mode of living."

Matthew smiled. "I know you will. Now go to the Underworld."

Miles didn't look back as he traveled to the Underworld. This dark world that lay deep beneath the surface was the most horrifying and inhospitable terrain Miles had ever encountered. Pools of magma and lava lined the ground, and Miles walked carefully through this demonic world, searching for the famed Voodoo Demon.

He looked down at the hellstone, but remembered Matthew had told him that he wasn't prepared to mine for it yet, and extracting the valuable hellstone ore would inflict serious damage on him. He reminded himself that he was there to find the Voodoo Demon. However, the more he searched the Underworld, the more he believed he might never find it.

Miles was standing by a pool of lava, when a flying beast spawned in front of him. He instantly recognized this creature as the Voodoo Demon. The winged beast carried the coveted Guide Voodoo Doll by its talons. The precious doll hung inches from Miles as he leapt toward this vicious bird of prey.

"I want that doll!" Miles screamed, although speaking was pointless. This wasn't the way the Voodoo Demon communicated.

Miles narrowly avoided tripping into a pool of lava. He knew if he made one bad move, he'd be destroyed, creating a pointless battle with the challenging Voodoo Demon. He swiftly sprinted, leading the winged demon away from the lava, and struck the creature.

The Voodoo Demon let out a loud cry. Miles was shocked by the powerful sound. He quickly slammed his sword into the beast as it shrieked and disappeared, dropping the Guide Voodoo Doll. He picked up the doll and summoned the Wall of Flesh.

Miles walked over to the pool of lava and dropped the doll into the flaming pool. He winced as he placed the doll in the pool, knowing the minute it fell into the deep rich red lava that Matthew would disappear from his home, and would be placed as a guide with another person. Miles's eyes filled with tears as the doll was slowly engulfed in lava. He had successfully summoned the Wall of Flesh. But this wasn't a victorious event—it was the start of Miles's most demanding battle. He lost his best friend for this opportunity and he was going to win.

Miles wasn't prepared for the hideousness of the Wall of Flesh. Its enormous cylinder-shaped body had a large mouth full of pointy teeth and two eyes bulging from either side of the gaping mouth. Miles flew up in the sky with his rocket boots and shot arrows at the tall beast.

The beast shot a fiery laser from its eyes, and he flew higher to avoid getting hit, and grabbed his sword and struck the red vile being. With each arrow that pierced through the Wall of Flesh's body or eyes, the beast became increasingly agitated. Moving fast, it raced toward Miles, who shot another round of arrows.

Miles gasped, as the mouth floated from the belly of the beast. The mouth, which appeared to be its own entity, was attached to a vein connecting to the Wall of Flesh. The mouth chomped as it flew straight toward Miles. The rocket boots weren't powerful enough to escape the clutches of this gruesome mouth. The beast unleashed more fiery lasers, leaving Miles with little energy.

He clung to his sword, pounding into the Wall of Flesh, and finally weakening it. But the Wall of Flesh became more vicious as it grew weaker. Miles hit it harder, trying not to get killed, hoping his last attempt would annihilate the red bumpy being, which looked like raw meat.

Miles struck one of the eyes, as the Wall slowly faded. He threw a grenade at the mouth and struck the body. Miles used his sword to strike the beast in its state of vulnerability. For a second it felt like the world stood still. He wasn't sure what was happening.

A message appeared telling him ancient spirits were released. They were the spirits of light and darkness. He knew this signified he'd defeated the Wall of Flesh and was now on hardmode. He wanted to rush back and tell Matthew about his victory, but he remembered he was gone. He did recall Matthew's last piece of advice. Matthew said, "Once you defeat the wall of flesh, you must grab the Pwnhammer. Then you can travel back to The Corruption and break a demon altar. These are the benefits of hardcorde mode."

Miles saw a tiny room in the sky and went inside. There he found the Pwnhammer. He was ready to break a demon altar. Miles wanted to tell his friends about his victory. He also had to alert them that they were on hardmode. He worried, as he sprinted back to town, that they might be in the middle of attack by a new hostile enemy. As he raced home, he stopped when a voice called out from a large cavern.

Chapter 18:
NEXT LEVEL

Miles rushed into the cavern and saw a man who appeared to be bound against the wall, dressed in a purple robe. A pointy purple hat covered his grey hair and he had a long grey beard.

"Well, hi there!" he exclaimed.

"Who are you?" asked Miles.

"I'm Cedric. I'm a wizard," he said "You saved me."

"I bet you want me to build you a house now, right?" asked Miles.

"You're a smart kid."

Miles introduced himself and led Cedric out of the cavern. "I have to go back to my town. I'm sad though," he confessed. "I miss my guide."

"You learned all you can from him. I'm sure he's happily off educating another noob," Cedric said, but realized his words weren't filling the hole in Miles's heart. He tried a lighthearted approach and put his hand behind Miles's ear. "Wow! I found a coin behind your ear."

Miles laughed, "If you're a wizard, I bet you know a lot better magic tricks than that one."

"Are you saying that's a bad trick?"

"No, but I'd love to learn about real magic. Can you teach me?"

Cedric nodded. "Of course. I can teach you all sorts of tricks and spells. I also have a bunch of useful tools to perfect your ability to perform magic."

Miles was excited to introduce Cedric to his friends. As they approached the houses, Miles spotted John rushing toward them.

"You did it. We knew you'd defeat the Wall of Flesh," John called out. Everyone raced to Miles, and he introduced them to his new friend, Cedric.

The gang talked to Cedric, when Miles interrupted. "Cedric, I know you wanted me to build you a home, but I'd like to offer you this one." He walked toward Matthew's door. "This was my guide Matthew's house. If you'd like, you can live here."

"I'd be honored," Cedric said and walked into the house. "It's a fantastic house."

"Thanks," Miles replied. "It's right next door to mine."

"I am grateful to live here. And I promise to be your guide in the world of magic."

Isaac hollered, "Get out of the house. We have some celebrating to do."

Miles joined the others in celebration. As he told them a detailed account of his battle with the Wall of Flesh, Miles thought about Matthew. He hoped Matthew was happy with his new student. Miles knew he'd always miss Matthew and would never forget all of the important information he taught him. Matthew was a guide and a friend, which was an unforgettable combination.

THE END